Jade's Life Skills Series

Problem Solving
Or
Don't Push!

By Asaf Shani

Illustrated by
Louise Gale Budol

Jade sat in the living room, feeling upset. Dad opened the door. "Hi," he greeted Jade, with a smile. She didn't answer. Dad sat beside her on the sofa, put his hand on her shoulder, and asked, "What's wrong?" Holding back tears, Jade said, "My friend, Julian, wouldn't let me play with her new toy. She kept saying 'no'. I asked her so many times!" Dad opened his arms for a hug and Jade snuggled in. "It is upsetting getting 'no' for an answer," Dad said, and Jade nodded. Dad continued, "'No' is not the end of the line. In fact, it's the beginning of a conversation!" Jade lifted her head, listening.

"Hearing 'no' is like being pushed, isn't it?" Dad asked. Jade thought about this. "It's like a push with words and not with hands," she agreed. Dad said, "I'll tell you about a guy named Isaac Newton, who lived almost four hundred years ago in England." Jade looked puzzled and Dad continued, "After he was hit on the head by a falling apple, he wondered why apples always fall in a straight line. He discovered many physical laws that govern our world, like gravity and the motion of objects.

"One of the laws Newton discovered was that if you push something, it will push you back." Dad demonstrated a constant light pressure on Jade's shoulder with his hand. "I'm pushing your body and, you'll notice that your body is resisting my push. This is Newton's third law of physics." Jade sat silent and concentrated on what Dad was saying. "Talking to people follows the same rule. If someone says 'no' to you, it feels like a push." Jade said, "Then I want to push back!" Dad nodded. "Exactly. Then what happens?" "Then we argue," said Jade. Dad nodded. "That is what happens when people start pushing."

"Wait a minute," Dad said and got up from the sofa. He returned after a few minutes wearing a red wig with pigtails. He'd even dotted his face so it looked like he had freckles. Jade started laughing. "Hi," Dad said in a child's voice "My name is Julian." Jade continued laughing. "Let's pretend we're having the same conversation you had with Julian," Dad said in his normal tone. "I'll be her, and you'll be yourself, okay?" Jade nodded and, with a smile, turned to Dad and asked, "Julian, please may I play with your new toy?" In a kid's voice, Dad said, "No." Jade scowled. "Then I won't be your friend!" she said.

Jade's eyes filled with tears. Dad made a timeout sign with his hands and hugged Jade. He said, "That was quite upsetting." Jade nodded. "Do you see how you and Julian got into a pushing cycle? Julian's 'no' was like a push, and then you pushed back by saying you wouldn't be her friend." Jade thought for a while and then nodded again. Dad asked, "Why did Julian say 'no'?" Jade answered, "She was afraid I'd break her new toy." "Did you actually hear her say that, or is that what you think?" Jade replied, "That's what I think ..." Dad touched the tip of her nose and said with a smile, "The way to stop the pushing cycle is by asking the other person a question. Ask them why they said 'no'."

"Let's do another exercise," Dad suggested. "Ask me for something, anything." Jade frowned as she thought what to ask. "Dad, can I have ice cream?" "No! You can't," Dad said immediately. "But Dad," Jade quickly answered, "it's my favorite thing!" Dad said, "My answer is still no." "You're mean!" Jade said. Dad smiled and made the timeout sign again. He said, "We got into a pushing cycle again." Jade nodded.

Dad said, "The influence of Newton's third law on humans is very strong. The good news is that we can train ourselves to break the pushing cycle or, even better, not to get into one." "How?" Jade asked. Dad answered, "First let me tell you the story of Jerry the fox and his fight for grapes. Then I'll teach you four steps for solving problems."

Jade nodded and Dad started the story. "Jerry the fox loved grapes. Unfortunately, the grape vines were surrounded by a high fence of prickly cactuses. Jerry waited impatiently for weeks until the grapes were ripe. When they were red and juicy, he trotted to the cactus fence. His mouth watered as he imagined the taste of the grapes.

"Jerry tried to push his paws between the cactuses but the prickles jabbed him, and his fur got caught. Jerry felt hungry, annoyed, and upset! He fetched a stick and tried to push the cactuses aside, but the stick broke. Jerry stared at the cactuses with narrowed eyes. You are in my way, he thought! He didn't notice that Samuel the badger had walked up and was staring curiously at him.

"Jerry ground his teeth in anger, and looked around for something else he could use. 'Say,' said Samuel, 'what are ya doing?' 'Can't you see I'm busy?' said Jerry in an angry tone. He picked up a stone and was about to throw it at the cactuses when Samuel asked, '**Why** do you want to throw this stone?' 'Shhh!!!' said Jerry grumpily. He threw the stone at the cactuses, hoping to punch a hole through. But when the stone hit them, the flexible cactuses swung back and Jerry got a headful of prickles! 'Ouch!' he cried in pain. 'Maybe I can help?' offered Samuel but Jerry rubbed his head and said, 'No, you can't!'

"Jerry picked up a much longer stick, planning to use it to high jump over the cactuses. Samuel watched as he started running towards the plants. But as Jerry was lifting in the air, the stick snapped and Jerry fell, butt first, on the cactuses. "Ouch!' he cried as he lay on the ground. Tears of frustration ran down his cheeks.

'Ah! I get it!' said Samuel suddenly. "You're trying to get to the grapes." He laid a paw on his friend's shoulder. "Please get up," he said. When Jerry was standing, Samuel led the way through a hole hidden between the cactuses, and handed him a bunch of sweet grapes. "'Next time,' said Samuel with an encouraging smile, 'tell me WHY you're trying to do something and maybe I can save you from the prickles.' Jerry put a grape in his mouth; it tasted delicious."

Dad smiled at Jade. "Jerry was in a pushing cycle with plants and with his good friend, Samuel!" Jade giggled. "Next time you're in a pushing cycle, ask yourself if you want to have the prickles or the grapes. The only way to avoid the prickles is to ask the question 'why?'" Jade thought about Julian. "When she said 'no' to me, and then I was mean back, we were like prickly things," Jade said. "We were hurting each other because we were pushing against each other. Asking 'why' is like looking for the hole in the fence." Dad smiled. "Nicely said! Most people regard 'no' as a wall. Asking 'why' may easily create a door in that wall."

Dad continued, "There are four steps to prevent getting into a prickly pushing match with someone and get what you want instead. First, notice that you and the other person are sliding into a pushing cycle. Second, act like a detective and ask them 'why' they are pushing you. Third, listen to their answer—with the detective hat on your head, find out what the other person DOES want. Finally, step four; ask them how what both of you want can be achieved."

Jade frowned. Dad smiled. "Let's try the model on your request for ice-cream." Jade nodded. "Just a minute," Dad said, got up from the sofa, and returned a few minutes later with sheets of paper. He did a 'come on' gesture with his hand—inviting Jade to ask for ice-cream.

Jade asked, "Dad, can I have some ice-cream?" "No!" Dad answered. Jade was about to answer back when Dad lifted a sheet a paper with a drawing of a road that forked. One road led to prickles and the other to the grapes. Jade smiled and swallowed what she was about to say. Dad held up another drawing. On it was a detective hat. Jade smiled and asked, "Why can't I have ice cream?" Dad answered, "Because I don't want you to eat too much unhealthy food—too many sweets." Dad lifted the third drawing with an image of the detective hat and a No turning into a Yes.

Jade thought about it and said, "You DON'T want me to eat too much unhealthy food ..." Dad nodded in excitement ... "So, you DO want me to eat more healthy food." Dad raised his thumb and showed Jade the last drawing. On it were pictures of Dad and Jade and in between them the word 'AND'. "So," Jade tried, "how can I eat more healthy food AND have a serving of ice cream?"

Dad clapped his hands. "Well done!" he said, and Jade smiled with pride. "You can have a serving of ice cream now if you promise to finish all of your veggies at dinner," Dad offered. Jade smiled and nodded. Dad held out a hand to Jade. "Let's shake on it!"

The next day, Jade and Julian were playing. "Can I play with your toy?" Jade asked. "No!" Julian answered. Jade was about to answer back but then she remembered Jerry and his fight with the cactuses. She could see in her mind's eye a road that forked. One road led to prickles and the other to the grapes. "Why won't you let me play with your toy?" she asked.

"Because you might dirty it," Julian answered. Jade thought, What Julian is saying is ... she DOESN'T want her toy to get dirty so she DOES want it to stay clean! Jade said, "How can we keep your toy clean AND play with it together?" Julian was silent. Her eyes moved as she thought of an answer. "I know!" she said. "Let's both go and wash our hands!" Jade smiled and nodded. "Okay!"

"Dad?" Jade said when she got home from Julian's. "Yes?" Dad said, lifting his eyes from the newspaper. "Your four steps to solve a problem work great! I used them with Julian, and guess what? She let me play with her new toy." Jade smiled in satisfaction. Dad grinned and said, "I knew you could do it!"

21

The End

Made in the USA
Middletown, DE
08 July 2023